Welcome to the Forest, where
**THE MINISTRY OF MONSTERS**
helps humans and monsters live side
by side in peace and harmony...

**CONNOR O'GOYLE**
lives here too, with his gargoyle mum,
human dad and his dog, Trixie.
But Connor's no ordinary boy...

When monsters get out of control,
Connor's the one for the job.
He's half-monster, he's the Ministry's
**NUMBER ONE AGENT**,
and he's licensed to do things
no one else can do. He's...

# MONSTER BOY!

For William Ingleby-Lewis

First published in 2009 by Orchard Books
First paperback publication in 2010

ORCHARD BOOKS
338 Euston Road, London NW1 3BH
*Orchard Books Australia*
Level 17/207 Kent St, Sydney, NSW 2000

ISBN 978 1 40830 243 9 (hardback)
ISBN 978 1 40830 251 4 (paperback)

Text and illustrations © Shoo Rayner 2009

The right of Shoo Rayner to be identified as the author and
illustrator of this work has been asserted by him in accordance with the
Copyright, Designs and Patents Act, 1988.

A CIP catalogue record for this book is available from the British Library.

1 3 5 7 9 10 8 6 4 2 (hardback)
1 3 5 7 9 10 8 6 4 2 (paperback)

Printed in Great Britain

Orchard Books is a division of Hachette Children's Books,
an Hachette UK company.

www.hachette.co.uk

# WEREWOLF WAIL

## SHOO RAYNER

ORCHARD BOOKS

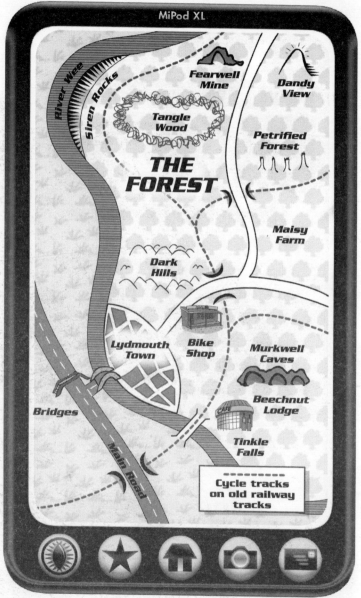

"Yarrooow-ow-ow-owl!" A loud, eerie, moaning howl rattled the window frames. The lights flickered. China tinkled on the sideboard.

YARROOOW-OW-OW-OWL!

Trixie whimpered and fluttered up to her basket on top of the bookcase. She hid her face in her paws.

"Mr Howler, our teacher, says it's a full moon tonight," Connor told his mum. "He says the moon brings out the worst in monsters."

"That's unkind to monsters," said Mum. "The moon brings out the worst in people, too." She pointed at the TV. "Turn it up will you, dear? I can't hear what they're saying with all that howling outside."

Connor pressed the remote control. The newsreader was reporting a Lunar Crime Wave.

"It's a full moon, so you'd better stay inside and lock your doors. The Police Chief says that crime is set to soar in town tonight."

The Police Chief appeared on the screen. "Criminals love the full moon," he explained. "The moonlight helps them see where they are going. Stay indoors and be safe."

"I'm glad we don't live in town," said Mum.

Connor's MiPod beeped. He flipped it open and read the message.

# MISSION ALERT!

| | |
|---|---|
| **To:** | Monster Boy, Number One Agent |
| **From:** | Mission Control, Ministry of Monsters |
| **Subject:** | Loud howling reported in the forest |

No one can sleep! It's a full moon, so it could be a Werewolf.

Please investigate immediately.

Good luck!

M.O.M.

## THIS MESSAGE WILL SELF-ERASE IN FIFTEEN SECONDS

"I need MB3 with the Netalizer," Connor told his Mum.

"It'll be ready in five minutes." Mum rushed to the hidden store where she looked after Connor's top-secret Monster Bikes.

"Come on, Trixie," Connor called up to his pet dog. "We've got work to do."

But Trixie didn't want to go out. Not tonight. The howling made her nervous.

"I know how to get you down," said Connor. He fetched a box of Doggo Chocs and shook it.

Dogs just can't resist them!

Trixie sat up, wagged her tail, spread her wings and flew into Connor's arms. She devoured one of the chocolate treats.

"Exactly like it says on the packet," Connor smiled to himself. "Dogs just can't resist them!"

**Doggo Chocs**

*Dogs just can't resist them!*

"Be careful," said Mum. "I don't really like you going out at night."

"I'll be fine," said Connor. "The moon's as bright as day."

Connor's mum was a Gargoyle, so Connor was half-monster. His code-name was Monster Boy. If anyone could look after himself, Connor could.

Connor put Trixie in her basket on the handlebars. "Anyway, I've got Trixie to look after me."

"Wuff!" said Trixie, snaffling another Doggo Choc.

"I've packed your sandwiches and a flask of hot milk," said Mum. "You'd better take the Doggo Chocs, too."

PEDAL-

"Thanks, Mum." Connor straddled the bike and set off into the starry moonlit night.

# MONSTER BIKE INFO

### MB3

MB3 is capture bike. It has many attachments to suit different monsters.

The Netalizer is a square net held up by gas-powered poles. When the poles collapse, the net falls on the monster. The net is drawn tight into an escape-proof bag.

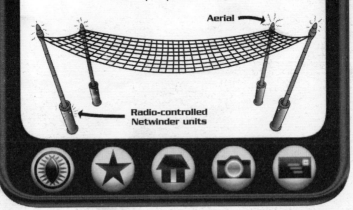

Aerial ➤

Radio-controlled Netwinder units

It wasn't a difficult case for Connor. He just followed the howling noise. Soon he could see the culprit, silhouetted against the enormous yellow moon.

"The Ministry was right," Connor whispered. "It's a Werewolf."

YOWL-YOWL-YOWL-YOWL

Trixie growled. Normally she liked chasing monsters, but Werewolves were different!

Connor unpacked the Netalizer and began setting it up. "Now all we have to do is get him into the trap," he thought out loud.

Connor inched MB3 closer to the Werewolf. In a small clearing, Connor could see a hairy, human-shaped, wolfish creature. It had lost its human clothes. Now it danced and howled at the moon in just a vest and a pair of underpants!

Connor's MiPod vibrated silently in his pocket. Connor looked at the screen.

It was a message from his dad, Gary O'Goyle, the world-famous Mountain Bike Champion. He always sent messages at the most unhelpful times!

# Frankfurt 200 km

Hi son,

Just won the Frankfurt 200 km Gourmet Mountain Bike Challenge.

I had to eat a different gourmet sausage every kilometre... Hic! Burp!

Lots of love,
Dad

"Thanks, Dad," Connor whispered.
"That gives me an idea."

Connor placed a Doggo Choc into the launch tube at the front of MB3. He flipped up the lid of the bell and pressed a glowing red button.

With a quiet *whump!*
the Doggo Choc flew
through the air and
landed at the feet of
the Werewolf.

"Huh?" The Werewolf stopped howling. It picked up the Doggo Choc, sniffed it, put it in its mouth and began to chew.

"Mmmm! Yum!" The Werewolf rubbed its tummy.

"Exactly like the packet says," Connor smiled to himself, as he loaded the launcher again. "Dogs just can't resist them!"

He aimed a few metres away from the Werewolf and *whump!* – another Doggo Choc flew through the air.

The Werewolf lurched forwards, picked it up and ate it.

*Whump! Whump! Whump!*
Connor laid down a trail of
Doggo Chocs. The last one
landed right underneath
the Netalizer.

The greedy Werewolf followed the trail until he was crouching under the net, eating the last Doggo Choc.

Connor pressed the glowing green button on his handlebar control unit.

*Pishhhh!* The gas-powered rods collapsed. The net fell. The Netalizer drew itself together like a monster string bag. It was so strong that nothing could escape once it was caught inside.

The howling stopped. There was nothing more for Connor to do but go back home and wait until morning.

# MiPOD MONSTER IDENTIFIER PROGRAM

**Monster:**

Werewolf

**Distinguishing Features:**
Wolf-like appearance, large teeth and loud wail.

**Preferred Habitat:**
Anywhere under a full moon.

**Essential Information:**
Some humans turn into Werewolves when there is a full moon. Often they lose their clothes when they transform. This can be embarrassing when they become human again in the morning!

**Danger Rating:** 3.5

"Right," said Connor, bright and early the next morning. "Let's see who this Werewolf really is."

The thing under the net had lost all its wolfy hair. Connor pressed the release button.

*Pishhhh!* The Netalizer poles raised the net up in the air, leaving a huddled human shape on the ground.

"Mr Howler!" Connor exclaimed.

It was Connor's teacher – in his vest and underpants!

"Y-y-y-you've got to help me," Mr Howler stammered. "I'm afraid I might lose my job if anyone finds out I'm a Werewolf. I'm supposed to be a responsible human being!"

"I've got an idea, sir," said Connor, as
he scouted ahead, making sure no one
saw his teacher dart from tree to tree on
his way back home.

"Five merit points if your idea is any good," said Mr Howler.

"Well," Connor explained, "I don't think people would mind if they knew you were a responsible Werewolf. Have you ever thought of doing a part-time evening job?"

A month later, the full moon passed quietly in the Forest. No howling, no wailing. Everyone woke up in a good mood after a great night's sleep.

ZZZZZZZZZ

On the TV news, the Police Chief was smiling.

FONY

"There has been a dramatic fall in full-moon crime. I'm glad to report that criminals have decided to stay in bed rather than meet Special Constable Howler on his midnight patrol. Constable Howler's policing methods are unusual and a little bit noisy, but they are extremely effective."

During break time at school that morning, Mr Howler looked tired.

"You look like you've been up all night, sir," Connor said, with a wink.

"I have!" his teacher replied. "It's hard work being a part-time Special Constable, Connor, but it's worth it. Everyone is happy now. Your idea was certainly worth five merit points!"

"Thank you, sir." Connor held out a box. "Here's a present from Trixie. She's really pleased you've stopped all your howling."

Mr Howler was surprised.
He opened the box and
looked inside. A broad grin
spread across his face.

"Doggo Chocs!" he
laughed. "Mmmm –
I just can't resist them!"

**SHOO RAYNER**
# MONSTER BOY

### All priced at £3.99

The Monster Boy stories are available from all good bookshops,
or can be ordered direct from the publisher:
Orchard Books, PO BOX 29, Douglas IM99 1BQ
Credit card orders please telephone 01624 836000
or fax 01624 837033 or visit our website: www.orchardbooks.co.uk
or e-mail: bookshop@enterprise.net for details.

To order please quote title, author and ISBN
and your full name and address.
Cheques and postal orders should be made payable to 'Bookpost plc.'
Postage and packing is FREE within the UK
(overseas customers should add £2.00 per book).

Prices and availability are subject to change.